Medusa's Coil

Z. B. Bishop & H. P. Lovecraft

Pharos Books

HB ISBN: 978-93-71417-94-5
ISBN: 978-93-59831-39-8
eISBN: 978-93-59830-12-4

Publisher: Pharos Books (P) Ltd.
Plot No.-63, 1st Floor, Main Mother Dairy Road
Pandav Nagar, East Delhi-110092
Phone: 011-40395855, +4049916623
WhatsApp: +91 9319228272
E-mail: bookspharos@gmail.com
Website: www.pharosbooks.in
Edition: 2025

Printed By: Sushma Book Binding House, Okhla Industrial Area, Phase II, New Delhi-110020

Medusa's Coil
Z. B. Bishop & H. P. Lovecraft

A powerful and compelling tale of brooding horror that deepens and broadens to the final catastrophe—an unusual and engrossing novelette by the author of "The Curse of Yig."

Medusa's Coil

The drive toward Cape Girardeau had been through unfamiliar country; and as the late afternoon light grew golden and half dream-like I realized that I must have directions if I expected to reach the town before night. I did not care to be wandering about these bleak southern Missouri lowlands after dark, for roads were poor and the November cold rather formidable in an open roadster. Black clouds, too, were massing on the horizon; so I looked about among the long gray and blue shadows that streaked the flat, brownish fields, hoping to glimpse some house where I might get the needed information.

It was a lonely and deserted country, but at last I spied a roof among a clump of trees near the small river on my right; perhaps a full half-mile from the road, and probably reachable by some path or drive upon which I would presently come. In the absence of any nearer dwelling, I resolved to try my luck there; and was glad when the bushes by the roadside revealed the ruin of a carved stone gateway, covered with dry, dead vines and choked with undergrowth which explained why I had not been able to trace the path across the fields in my first distant view. I saw that I could not drive the car in; so I parked it very carefully near the gate—where a thick evergreen would shield it in case of rain—and got out for the long walk to the house.

Traversing that brush-grown path in the gathering twilight I was conscious of a distinct sense of foreboding, probably induced by the air of sinister decay hovering about the gate and the former driveway. From the carvings on the old stone pillars I inferred that this place was once an estate of manorial dignity; and I could clearly see that the driveway had originally boasted guardian lines of linden trees, some of which had died, while others had lost their special identity among the wild scrub growths of the region.

As I plowed onward, cockleburrs and stickers clung to my clothes, and I began to wonder whether the place could be inhabited after all. Was I tramping on a vain errand? For a moment I was tempted to go back and try some farm farther along the road, when a view of the house ahead aroused my curiosity and stimulated my venturesome spirit.

There was something provocatively fascinating in the tree-girt, decrepit pile before me, for it spoke of the graces and spaciousness of a bygone era and a far more southerly environment. It was a typical wooden plantation house of the classic, early Nineteenth Century pattern, with two and a half stories and a great Ionic portico whose pillars reached up as far as the attic and supported a triangular pediment. Its state of decay was extreme and obvious: one of the vast columns having rotted and fallen to the ground, while the upper piazza or balcony had sagged dangerously low. Other buildings, I judged, had formerly stood near it.

As I mounted the broad stone steps to the low porch and the carved and four-lighted doorway I felt distinctly nervous, and started to light a cigarette—desisting when I saw how dry and inflammable everything about me was. Though now convinced that the house was deserted, I nevertheless hesitated to violate its dignity without knocking; so I tugged at the rusty iron knocker until I could get it to move, and finally set up a cautious rapping which seemed to make the whole place shake and rattle. There was no response; yet once more I plied the cumbrous, creaking device, as much to dispel the sense of unholy silence and solitude as to arouse any possible occupant of the ruin.

Somewhere near the river I heard the mournful note of a dove, and it seemed as if the coursing water itself were faintly audible. Half in a dream, I seized and rattled the ancient latch, and finally gave the great six-paneled door a frank trying. It was unlocked, as I could see in a moment; and though it stuck and grated on its hinges I began to push it open, stepping through it into a vast shadowy hall as I did so.

But the moment I took this step I regretted it. It was not that a legion of specters confronted me in that dim and dusty hall with the ghostly Empire furniture, but that I knew at once that the place was not deserted after all. There was a creaking on the great curved staircase, and the sound of faltering footsteps slowly descending. Then I saw a tall, bent figure silhouetted for an instant against the great Palladian window on the landing.

My first terror was soon over, and as the figure descended the final flight I was ready to greet the house-holder whose privacy I had invaded. In the semi-darkness I could see him reach into his pocket for a match. There came a flare as he lighted a small kerosene lamp which stood on a rickety console table near the foot of the stairs. The feeble glow revealed the stooping figure of a very tall, emaciated old man, disordered in dress and unshaven as to face, yet for all that with the bearing and expression of a gentleman.

I did not wait for him to speak, but at once began to explain my presence.

"You'll pardon my coming in like this, but when my knocking didn't raise anybody I concluded that no one lived here. I wanted to know the shortest road to Cape Girardeau. I wanted to get there before dark, but now, of course—"

As I paused, the man spoke, in exactly the cultivated tone I had expected, and with a mellow accent as unmistakably Southern as the house he inhabited.

"Rather, you must pardon me for not answering your knock more promptly. I live in a very retired way, and am not usually expecting visitors. At first I thought you were a mere curiosity-seeker. When you knocked again I started to answer, but I am not well and have to move very slowly, owing to spinal neuritis—very troublesome case.

"As for your getting to town before dark—you can't do that. The road you are on isn't the best or shortest way. What you must do is to take the first real road to your left after you leave the gate. There are three or four cart-paths you can ignore, but you can't mistake the real road because of the large willow tree on the right just opposite it.

"When once you've turned, keep on past two roads and turn to the right along the third. After that—"

Perplexed by these elaborate directions, confusing indeed to a total stranger, I could not help interrupting.

"Please, how can I follow all these clues in pitch-darkness, without ever having been near here before, and with only an indifferent pair of headlights to tell me what is and what isn't a road? Besides, I think it's going to storm pretty soon, and my car is an open one. It looks as if I were in a bad fix if I want to get to Cape Girardeau tonight. The fact is, I don't think I'd better try. I don't like to impose, but in view of the circumstances, do you suppose you could put me up for the night? I won't be any trouble. Just let me have a corner to sleep in till daylight, and I'm all right. I can leave the car in the road where it is; wet weather won't hurt it."

As I made my sudden request I could see the old man's face lose its former expression of quiet resignation and take on an odd, surprised look.

"Sleep *here*?"

He seemed so astonished at my request that I repeated it.

"Yes, why not? I assure you I won't be any trouble. What else can I do? I'm a stranger hereabouts, these roads are a labyrinth in the dark, and I'll wager it'll be raining torrents inside of an hour——"

This time it was my host's turn to interrupt, and as he did so I could feel a peculiar quality in his deep, musical voice.

"A stranger—of course you must be, else you wouldn't think of sleeping here; wouldn't think of coming here at all. People don't come here nowadays."

He paused, and my desire to stay was increased a thousandfold by the sense of mystery his laconic words seemed to evoke. There was something queer about this place, and the pervasive musty smell seemed to cloak a thousand secrets. Again I noticed the extreme decrepitude of everything about me; manifest even in the feeble rays of the single small lamp. I felt woefully chilly, and saw with regret that no heating seemed to be provided; yet so great was my curiosity that I still wished most ardently to stay and learn something of the recluse and his dismal abode.

"You may stay if you really wish to; you can come to no harm that I know of. Others claim there are certain peculiarly undesirable influences here. As for me, I stay because I have to."

With my curiosity still more heightened, I prepared to take my host at his word, and followed him slowly upstairs when he motioned me to do so. It was very dark now, and faint pattering outside told me that the threatened rain had come. I would have been glad of any shelter, but this was doubly welcome because of the hints of mystery about the place and its master. For an incurable lover of the grotesque, no more fitting haven could have been provided.

There was a second-floor corner room in less unkempt shape than the rest of the house, and into this my host led me, setting down his small lamp and lighting a somewhat larger one. From the cleanliness and contents of the room, and from the books ranged along the walls, I could see that I had not guessed amiss in thinking the man a gentleman of taste and breeding. He was a hermit and eccentric, no doubt, but still had standards and intellectual interests. As he waved me to a seat I began a conversation on general topics, and was pleased to find him not at all taciturn. If anything, he seemed glad of someone to talk to, and did not attempt to swerve the discourse from personal topics.

He was, I learned, one Antoine de Russy, of an ancient, powerful and cultivated line of Louisiana planters. More than a century ago his grandfather, a younger son, had migrated to southern Missouri and founded a new estate in the lavish ancestral manner; building this pillared mansion and surrounding it with all the accessories of a great plantation. There had been, at one time, as many as two hundred negroes in the cabins which stood on the flat ground in the rear—ground that the river had now invaded—and to hear them singing and laughing and playing the banjo at night was to know the fullest charm of a civilization and social order now sadly extinct. In front of the house, where the great guardian oaks and willows stood, there had been a lawn like a broad green carpet, always watered and trimmed and with flag-stoned, flower-bordered walks curving through it. Riverside (for such the place was called) had been a lovely and idyllic homestead in its day; and my host could recall it when many traces of its best period still lingered.

It was raining hard now, with dense sheets of water beating against the insecure roof, walls, and windows, and sending in drops through a thousand chinks and crevices. Moisture trickled down to the floor from unsuspected places, and the mounting wind rattled the rotting, loose-hinged shutters outside. But I minded none of this, nor even thought of my roadster outside beneath the trees, for I saw that a story was coming. Incited to reminiscence, my host made a move to show me to sleeping-quarters, but kept on recalling older, better days. Soon, I saw, I might learn why he lived alone in that ancient place, and why his neighbors thought it full of undesirable influences. His voice was very musical as he spoke on, and his tale soon took a turn which left me no chance to grow drowsy.

"Yes, Riverside was built in 1816, and my father was born here in 1828. He died young, so young I can just barely remember him. In '64, he was killed in the war—Seventh Louisiana Infantry, C.S.A.—for he went back to the old home to enlist. My grandfather was too old to fight, yet he lived on to be ninety-five, and helped my mother bring me up: good bringing-up, too, I'll give them credit. We always had strong traditions, high notions of honor, and my grandfather saw to it that I grew up the way de Russys have grown up, generation after generation, ever since the Crusades. We weren't quite wiped out financially, and managed to get on very comfortably after the war. I went to a good school in Louisiana, and later to Princeton. Later on I was able to get the plantation on a fairly profitable basis, though you see what it's come to now.

"My mother died when I was twenty, and my grandfather two years later. It was rather lonely after that; and in '85 I married a distant cousin in New Orleans. Things might have been different if she'd lived, but she died when my son Denis was born. Then I had only Denis. I didn't try marriage again, but gave all my time to the boy. He was like me, like all the de Russys, darkish and tall and thin, and with the devil of a temper. I gave him the same training my grandfather had given me, but he didn't need much training when it came to points of honor. It was in him. Never saw such high spirit—all I could do to keep him from running away to the Spanish War when he was eleven! Romantic young devil, too full of high notions—you'd call 'em Victorian, now—no trouble at all to make him let the nigger wenches alone. I sent him to the same school I'd gone to, and to Princeton, too. He was Class of 1909.

"In the end he decided to be a doctor, and went a year to the Harvard Medical School. Then he hit on the idea of keeping to the old French tradition of the family, and argued me into sending him to the Sorbonne. I did—and proudly enough, though I knew how lonely I'd be with him so far off. Would to God I hadn't! I thought he was the safest kind of a boy to be in Paris. He had a room in the Rue St. Jacques—that's near the University in the Latin Quarter—but according to his letters and his friends he didn't cut up with the gayer dogs at all. The people he knew were mostly young fellows from home—serious students and artists who thought more of their work than of striking attitudes and painting the town red.

"But of course there were lots of fellows who were on a sort of dividing line between serious study and the devil: the esthetes, the decadents, experimenters in life and sensation; the Baudelaire kind of a chap. Naturally, Denis ran up against a good many of these, and saw a good deal of their life. They had all sorts of crazy circles and cults—imitation devil-worship, false Black Masses, and the like. Doubt if it did them much harm on the whole—probably most of 'em forgot all about it in a year or two. One of the deepest in this queer stuff was a fellow Denis had known at school—for that matter, whose father I'd known myself. Frank Marsh, of New Orleans. Disciple of Lafcadio Hearn and Gauguin and Van Gogh—regular epitome of the yellow nineties. Poor devil—he had the makings of a great artist, at that.

"Marsh was the oldest friend Denis had in Paris; so as a matter of course they saw a good deal of each other, to talk over old times at St. Clair Academy, and all that. The boy wrote me a good deal about him, and I didn't see any especial harm when he spoke of the group of mystics Marsh ran with. It seems there was some cult of prehistoric Egyptian and Carthaginian magic having a rage among the Bohemian element on the left bank; some nonsensical thing that pretended to reach back to forgotten sources of hidden truth in lost African civilizations—the great Zimbabwe, and dead Atlantean cities in the Hoggar region of the Sahara—and that had a lot of gibberish connected with snakes and human hair. At least, I called it gibberish then. Denis used to quote Marsh as saying odd things about the veiled facts behind the legend of Medusa's snaky locks—and behind the later Ptolemaic myth of Berenice, who offered up her hair to save her husband-brother, and had it set in the sky as the constellation Coma Berenices.

"I don't think this business made much impression on Denis until the night of the queer ritual at Marsh's rooms when he met the priestess. Most of the devotees of this cult were young fellows, but the head of it was a young woman who called herself *Tanit-Isis*, letting it be know that her real name—her name in this latest incarnation, as she put it—was Marceline Bedard. She claimed to be the left-handed daughter of Marquis de Chameaux, and seemed to have been both a petty artist and an artist's model before adopting this more lucrative magical profession. Someone said she had lived for a time in the West Indies—Martinique, I think—but she was very reticent about herself. Part of her pose was a great show of austerity and holiness, but I don't think the more experienced students took that very seriously.

"Denis, though, was far from experienced, and wrote me fully ten pages of slush about the goddess he had discovered. If I'd only realized his simplicity I might have done something, but I never thought a puppy infatuation like that could mean much. I felt absurdly sure that Denis' touchy personal honor and family pride would always keep him out of the most serious complications.

"As time went on, though, his letters began to make me nervous. He mentioned this Marceline more and more, and his friends less and less; and began talking about the 'cruel and silly way' they declined to introduce her to their mothers and sisters. He seems to have asked her no questions about herself, and I don't doubt but that she filled him full of romantic legendry concerning her origin and divine revelations and the way people slighted her. At length I could see that Denis was altogether cutting his own crowd and spending the bulk of his time with this alluring priestess. At her especial request he never told the old crowd of their continual meetings; so nobody over there tried to break the affair up.

"I suppose she thought he was fabulously rich; for he had the air of a patrician, and people of a certain class think all aristocratic Americans are wealthy. In any case, she probably thought this a rare chance to contract a genuine right-handed alliance with a really eligible young man. By the time my nervousness burst into open advice, it was too late. The boy had lawfully married her, and wrote that he was dropping his studies and bringing the woman to Riverside. He said she had made a great sacrifice and resigned her leadership of the magical cult, and that henceforth she would be merely a private gentlewoman—the future mistress of Riverside, and mother of de Russys to come.

"Well, sir, I took it the best way I could. I knew that sophisticated Continentals have different standards from our old

American ones, and anyway, I really knew nothing against the woman. A charlatan, perhaps, but why necessarily any worse? I suppose I tried to keep as naïve as possible about such things in those days, for the boy's sake. Clearly, there was nothing for a man of sense to do but to let Denis alone so long as his new wife conformed to de Russy ways. Let her have a chance to prove herself—perhaps she wouldn't hurt the family as much as some might fear. So I didn't raise any objections or ask any penitence. The thing was done, and I stood ready to welcome the boy back, whatever he brought with him.

"They got here three weeks after the telegram telling of the marriage. Marceline was beautiful, and I could see how the boy might very well get foolish about her. She did have an air of breeding, and I think to this day she must have had some strain of good blood in her. She was apparently not much over twenty; of medium size, fairly slim, and as graceful as a tigress in posture and motions. Her complexion was a deep olive, and her eyes were large and very dark. She had small, classically regular features, though not quite clean-cut enough to suit my taste, and the most singular head of jet-black hair that I ever saw.

"I didn't wonder that she had dragged the subject of hair into her magical cult, for with that heavy profusion of it the idea must have occurred to her naturally. Coiled up, it made her look like some Oriental princess in a drawing of Aubrey Beardsley's. Hanging down her back, it came well below her knees and shone in the light as if it possessed some separate, unholy vitality of its own. I would almost have thought of Medusa or Berenice myself without having such things suggested to me, upon seeing and studying that hair.

"Sometimes I thought it moved slightly of itself, and tended to arrange itself in distinct ropes or strands, but this may have been sheer illusion. She brushed it incessantly, and seemed to use some sort of preparation on it. I got the notion once, a curious, whimsical notion, that it was a living thing which she had to feed in some strange way. All nonsense—but it added to my feeling of constraint about her and her hair.

"For I can't deny that I failed to like her wholly, no matter how hard I tried. Something about her repelled me subtly, and I could not help weaving morbid and macabre associations about everything connected with her. Her complexion called up thoughts of Babylon, Atlantis, Lemuria, and the terrible forgotten dominations of an elder world; her eyes struck me sometimes as the eyes of some unholy forest creature or animal-goddess too immeasurably ancient to be fully human; and her hair—that dense, exotic, overnourished growth of oily jet—made one shiver as a great black python might have done. There was no doubt but that she realized my involuntary attitude, though I tried to hide it, and she tried to hide the fact that she noticed it.

"Yet the boy's infatuation lasted. He positively fawned on her, and overdid all the little gallantries of daily life to a sickening degree. She appeared to return the feeling, though I could see it took a conscious effort to make her duplicate his enthusiasms and extravagances. For one thing, I think she was piqued to learn that we weren't as wealthy as she had expected.

"It was a bad business all told. I could see that sad undercurrents were arising. Denis was half hypnotized with puppy-love, and began to grow away from me as he felt my shrinking from his wife. This kind of thing went on for months, and I saw that I was losing my only son, the boy who had formed the center of all my thoughts and acts for the past quarter of a century.

"Marceline seemed to be a good wife enough in those early months, and our friends received her without any quibbling or questioning. I was always nervous, though, about what some of the young fellows in Paris might write home to their relatives after the news of the marriage spread around. Despite the woman's love of secrecy, it couldn't remain hidden forever; indeed Denis had written a few of his closest friends, in strict confidence, as soon as he was settled with her at Riverside.

"I got to staying more and more alone in my room with my failing health as an excuse. It was about that time that my present spinal neuritis began to develop. Denis didn't seem to notice the trouble, or take any interest in me and my habits and affairs; and it hurt me to see how callous he was getting. I began to get sleepless, and often racked my brain in the night to try to find out what really was the matter—what it really was that made my new daughter-in-law so repulsive and even dimly horrible to me.

"Oddly, the only ones who seemed to share my uneasiness were the servants. The darkies around the house seemed very sullen in their attitude toward her, and in a few weeks all save the few who were strongly attached to our family had left. These few—old Scipio and his wife Sarah, the cook Delilah, and Mary, Scipio's daughter, were as civil as possible, but plainly revealed that their new mistress commanded their duty rather than their affection. They stayed in their own remote part of the house as much as possible. McCabe, our white chauffeur, was insolently admiring rather than hostile; and another exception was a very old Zulu woman, said to have come from Africa over a hundred years before, who had been a sort of leader in her small cabin as a kind of family pensioner. Old Sophonisba always showed reverence whenever Marceline came near her, and one time I saw her kiss the ground where her mistress had walked. Blacks are superstitious animals, and I wondered whether Marceline had been talking any of her mystical nonsense to our hands in order to overcome their evident dislike.

"Well, that's how we went on for nearly half a year. Then, in the summer of 1916, things began to happen. Toward the middle of June Denis got a note from his old friend Frank Marsh, telling of a sort of nervous breakdown which made him want to take a rest in the country. It was post-marked New Orleans, for Marsh had gone home from Paris when he felt the collapse coming on, and seemed a very plain though polite bid for an invitation from us. Marsh, of course, knew that Marceline was here, and asked very courteously after her. Denis was sorry to hear of his trouble and told him at once to come along for an indefinite visit.

"Marsh came, and I was shocked to notice how he had changed since I had seen him in his earlier days. He was a smallish, lightish fellow, with blue eyes and an undecided chin; and now I could see the effects of drink and I don't know what else in his puffy eye-lids, enlarged nose-pores, and heavy lines around the mouth. I reckon he had taken his pose of decadence pretty seriously, and set out to be as much of a Rimbaud, Baudelaire, or Lautremont as he could. And yet he was delightful to talk to, for like all decadents he was exquisitely sensitive to the color and atmosphere and names of things; admirably, thoroughly alive, and with whole records of conscious experience in obscure, shadowy fields of living and feeling which most of us pass over without knowing they exist.

"I was glad of the visit, for I felt it would help to set up a normal atmosphere in the house again. And that's what it really seemed to do at first; for, as I said, Marsh was a delight to have around. He was as sincere and profound an artist as I ever saw in my life, and I certainly believe that nothing on earth mattered to him except the perception and expression of beauty. When he saw an exquisite thing, or was creating one, his eyes would dilate until the light irises went nearly out of sight, leaving two mystical black pits in that weak, delicate, chalk-like face; black pits opening on strange worlds which none of us could guess about.

"When he reached here, though, he didn't have any chances to show this tendency; for he had (as he told Denis) gone quite stale. It seems he had been very successful as an artist of a bizarre kind—like Fuseli or Goya or Sime or Clark Ashton Smith—but had suddenly become played out. The world of ordinary things around him had ceased to hold anything he could recognize as beauty of enough force and poignancy to arouse his creative faculty. He had often been this way before, but this time he could not invent any new, strange, or outré sensation or experience which would supply the needed illusion of fresh beauty or stimulating adventurous expectancy. He was like a Durtal or a des Esseintes at the most jaded point of his curious orbit.

"Marceline was away when Marsh arrived. She hadn't been enthusiastic about his coming, and had refused to decline an invitation from some of our friends in St. Louis which came about that time for her and Denis. Denis, of course, stayed to receive his guest, but Marceline had gone on alone. It was the first time they had ever been separated, and I hoped the interval would help dispel the sort of daze that was making such a fool of the boy. Marceline showed no hurry to get back, but seemed to me to prolong her absence as much as she could. Denis stood it better than one would have expected from such a doting husband, and seemed more like his old self as he talked over other days with Marsh and tried to cheer the listless esthete up.

"It was Marsh who seemed most impatient to see the woman; perhaps because he thought her strange beauty, or some phase of the mysticism which had gone into her one-time magical cult, might help to reawaken his interest in things and give him another start toward artistic creation. That there was no baser reason, I was absolutely certain from what I knew of Marsh's character. With all his weaknesses, he was a gentleman, and it had indeed relieved me when I first learned that he wanted to come here because his willingness to accept Denis' hospitality proved that there was no reason why he shouldn't.

"When, at last, Marceline did return, I could see that Marsh was tremendously affected. He did not attempt to make her talk of the bizarre thing which she had so definitely abandoned, but was unable to hide a powerful admiration which kept his eyes—now dilated in that curious way for the first time during his visit—riveted to her every moment she was in the room. She, however, seemed uneasy rather than pleased by his steady scrutiny; that is, she seemed so at first, though this feeling of hers wore away in a few days, and left the two on a basis of the most cordial and voluble congeniality. I could see Marsh studying her constantly when he thought no one was watching, and I wondered how long it would be that only the artist, and not the primitive man, would be aroused by her mysterious graces.

"Denis naturally felt some irritation at this turn of affairs; though he realized that his guest was a man of honor and that, as kindred mystics and esthetes, Marceline and Marsh would naturally have things and interests to discuss in which a more or less conventional person could have no part. He didn't hold anything against anybody, but merely regretted that his own imagination was too limited and traditional to let him talk with Marceline as Marsh talked. At this stage of things I began to see more of the boy. With his wife otherwise busy, he had time to remember that he had a father, who was ready to help him in any difficulty.

"We often sat together on the veranda watching Marsh and Marceline as they rode up or down the drive on horseback, or played tennis on the court that used to stretch south of the house. They talked mostly in French, which Marsh, though he hadn't more than a quarter-portion of French blood, handled more glibly than either Denis or I could speak it. Marceline's English, always academically correct, was rapidly improving in accent; but it was plain that she relished dropping back into her mother-tongue. As we looked at the congenial couple they made, I could see the boy's cheek and throat muscles tighten; though he wasn't a whit less ideal a host to Marsh, or a whit less considerate a husband to Marceline.

"All this was generally in the afternoon; for Marceline rose very late, had breakfast in bed, and took an immense amount of time preparing to come downstairs. It was in these morning hours that Denis and Marsh did their real visiting, and exchanged the close confidences which kept their friendship up despite the strain that jealousy imposed.

"Well, it was in one of those morning talks on the veranda that Marsh made the proposition which brought on the end. I was laid up, but had managed to get downstairs and stretch out on the front parlor sofa near the long window. Denis and Marsh were just outside; so I couldn't help hearing all they said. They had been talking about art, and the curious, capricious environmental elements needed to jolt an artist into producing work of merit, when Marsh suddenly swerved from abstractions to the personal application he must have had in mind from the start.

"'I suppose,' he was saying, 'that nobody can tell just what it is in some scenes or objects that makes them esthetic stimuli for certain individuals. Basically, of course, it must have some reference to each man's background of stored-up mental associations; for no two people have the same scale of sensitiveness and responses. For some of us all ordinary things have ceased to have any emotional or imaginative significance, but no one responds in the same way to exactly the same extraordinary thing. Now take me, for instance....

"'I know, Denny, that I can say these things to you because you have such a preternaturally unspoiled mind—clean, objective, and all that. You won't misunderstand. The fact is, I think I know what's needed to set my imagination working again. I've had a dim idea of it ever since we were in Paris, but I'm sure now. It's Marceline, old chap; that face and that hair, and the train of shadowy images they bring up. Not merely visible beauty—though God knows there's enough of that—but something peculiar and individualized, that can't exactly be explained. Do you know, in the last few days I've felt the existence of such a stimulus so keenly that I honestly think I could outdo myself, if I could get hold of paint and canvas at just the time when her face and hair set my fancy stirring and weaving.

"'There is something weird and other-worldly about it, something joined up with the dim ancient thing Marceline represents. I don't know how much she's told you about that side of her, but I can assure you there's plenty to it. She has some marvelous links with the outside.'

"Some change in Denis' expression must have halted the speaker here, for there was a considerable spell of silence before the words went on. I was utterly taken aback, for I'd expected no such overt development as this, and I wondered what my son could be thinking. My heart began to pound violently, and I strained my ears in the frankest of intentional eavesdropping. Then Marsh resumed.

"'Of course you're jealous—I know how a speech like mine must sound—but I can swear to you that you needn't be.'

"Denis did not answer, and Marsh went on.

"'To tell the truth, I could never be in love with Marceline—I couldn't even be a cordial friend of hers in the warmest sense. Why, damn it all, I feel like a hypocrite talking with her these days as I've been doing.

"'The case simply is, that one phase of her half hypnotizes me in a certain way—a very strange, fantastic, and dimly terrible way—just as another phase half hypnotizes you in a much more normal way. I see something in her—or to be psychologically exact, something through her or beyond her—that you don't see at all; something that brings up a vast pageantry of shapes from forgotten abysses, and makes me want to paint incredible things whose outlines vanish the instant I try to envisage them clearly. Don't mistake, Denny: your wife is a magnificent being, a splendid focus of cosmic forces who has a right to be called divine if anything on earth has!'

"I felt a clearing of the situation at this point, for the abstract strangeness of Marsh's expressed sentiment, plus the flattery he was now heaping on Marceline, could not fail to disarm and mollify one as fondly proud of his consort as Denis always was. Marsh evidently caught the change himself, for there was more confidence in his tone as he continued.

"'I must paint her, Denny, must paint that hair, and you won't regret it. There's something more than mortal about that hair, something more than beautiful——'

"He paused, and I wondered what Denis could be thinking. Was Marsh's interest actually that of the artist alone, or was he merely infatuated as Denis had been? I had thought, in their school days, that he had envied my boy, and I dimly felt that it might be the same now. On the other hand, something in that talk of artistic stimulus had rung amazingly true; so that the more

I pondered, the more I was inclined to take the stuff at face value. Denis seemed to do so, too, for although I could not catch his low-spoken reply, I could tell by the effect it produced that it must have been affirmative.

"There was a sound of someone slapping another on the back, and then a grateful speech from Marsh that I was long to remember.

"'That's great, Denny; and just as I told you, you'll never regret it. In a sense, I'm half doing it for you. You'll be a different man when you see it. It'll put you back where you used to be—give you a waking-up and a sort of salvation—but you can't see what I mean as yet. Just remember old friendship, and don't get the idea that I'm not the same old bird!'

"I rose perplexedly as I saw the two stroll off across the lawn, arm in arm. What could Marsh have meant by his strange and almost ominous reassurance? The more my fears were quieted in one direction, the mo re they were aroused in another. Look at it in any way I could, it seemed to be rather a bad business.

"But matters got started just the same. Denis fixed up an attic room with skylights, and Marsh sent for all sorts of painting equipment. Everyone was rather excited about the new venture, and I was at least glad that something was on foot to break the brooding tension.

"Soon the sittings began, and we all took them quite seriously, for we could see that Marsh regarded them as important artistic events. Denny and I used to go quietly about the house as though something sacred were occurring.

"With Marceline, though, it was a different matter, as I began to see at once. Whatever Marsh's reactions to the sittings may have been, hers were painfully obvious. Every possible way she betrayed a frank and commonplace infatuation for the artist, and would repulse Denis' marks of affection whenever she dared. Oddly, I noticed this more vividly than Denis himself, and tried to devise some plan for keeping the boy's mind easy until the matter could be straightened out. There was no use in having him excited about it if it could be helped.

"In the end I decided that Denis had better be away while the disagreeable situation existed. I could represent his interests well enough at this end, and sooner or later Marsh would finish the picture and go. My view of Marsh's honor was such that I did not look for any worse developments. When the matter had blown over, and Marceline had forgotten about her new infatuation, it would be time enough to have Denis on hand again.

"So I wrote a long letter to my marketing and financial agent in New York, and cooked up a plan to have the boy summoned there for an indefinite time. I had the agent write him that our affairs absolutely required one of us to go East, and of course my illness made it clear that I could not be the one. It was arranged that when Denis got to New York he would find enough plausible matters to keep him busy as long as I thought he ought to be away.

"The plan worked perfectly, and Denis started for New York without the least suspicion. Marceline and Marsh went with him in the car to Cape Girardeau, where he caught the afternoon train to St. Louis. They returned about dark, and as McCabe drove the car back to the stables I could hear them talking on the veranda. This time I resolved to do some intentional eavesdropping, so quietly went down to the front parlor and stretched out on the sofa near the window.

"At first I could hear nothing, but very shortly there came a sound as of a chair being shifted, followed by a short, sharp breath and a sort of inarticulately hurt exclamation from Marceline. Then I heard Marsh speaking in a strained, almost formal voice.

"'I'd enjoy working tonight—if you're not too tired.'

"Marceline's reply was in the same hurt tone which had marked her exclamation. She used English, as he had done.

"'Oh, Frank, is that really all you care about? Forever working! Can't we just sit out in this glorious moonlight?'

"He answered impatiently, his voice showing a certain contempt beneath the dominant quality of artistic enthusiasm.

"'Moonlight! Good God, what cheap sentimentality! For a supposedly sophisticated person you surely do hang on to some of the crudest claptrap that ever escaped from the dime novels. With art at your elbow, you have to think of the moon! Or perhaps it makes you think of the Roodmus dance around the stone pillars at Auteuil; hell! how you used to make those goggle-eyed yaps stare! But no, I suppose you've dropped all that now. No more Atlantean magic or hair-snake rites for Madame de Russy! I'm the only one to remember the old things, the things that came down through the temples of Tanit and called on the ramparts of Zimbabwe. But I won't be cheated of that remembrance—all that is weaving itself into the thing on my canvas—the thing that is going to capture wonder and crystallize the secrets of seventy-five thousand years.'

"Marceline interrupted in a voice full of mixed emotions.

"'It's you who are cheaply sentimental now! You know well that the old things had better be let alone. All of you had better look out if ever I chant the old rites or try to call up what lies hidden in Yuggoth, Zimbabwe, and Rl'yeh. I thought you had more sense!

"'You lack logic. You want me to be interested in this precious painting of yours, yet you never let me see what you're doing. Always that black cloth over it! It's of me—I shouldn't think it would matter if I saw it.'

"Marsh was interrupting this time, his voice curiously hard and strained.

"'No. Not now. You'll see it in due time. You say it's of you—yes, it's that, but it's more. If you knew, you mightn't be so impatient. Poor Denis! My God, it's a shame!'

"My throat went suddenly dry as the words rose to an almost febrile pitch. What could Marsh mean? Suddenly I saw that he had stopped and was entering the house alone. I heard the front door slam, and listened as his footsteps ascended the stairs.

Outside on the veranda I could still hear Marceline's heavy, angry breathing. I crept away sick at heart, feeling that there were grave things to ferret out before I could safely let Denis come back.

"After that evening the tension around the place was even worse than before. Marceline had always lived on flattery and fawning, and the shock of those few blunt words from Marsh was too much for her temperament.

"There was no living in the house with her any more, for with poor Denis gone she took out her abusiveness on everybody. When she could find no one indoors to quarrel with she would go out to Sophonisba's cabin and spend hours talking with the queer old Zulu woman. Aunt Sophy was the only person who would fawn abjectly enough to suit her, and when I tried once to overhear their conversation I found Marceline whispering about *elder secrets* and *unknown* Kadath while the Negress rocked to and fro in her chair, making inarticulate sounds of reverence and admiration every now and then.

"But nothing could break her dog-like infatuation for Marsh. She would talk bitterly and sullenly to him, yet was getting more and more obedient to his wishes. It was very convenient for him, since he now became able to make her pose for the picture whenever he felt like painting. He tried to show gratitude for this willingness, but I thought I could detect a kind of contempt or even loathing beneath his careful politeness. For my part, I frankly hated Marceline! There was no use in calling my attitude anything as mild as mere dislike these days. Certainly, I was glad Denis was away. His letters, not nearly so frequent as I wished, showed signs of strain and worry.

"As the middle of August went by I gathered from Marsh's remarks that the portrait was nearly done. His mood seemed increasingly sardonic, though Marceline's temper improved a bit, as the prospect of seeing the thing tickled her vanity. I can still recall the day when Marsh said he'd have everything finished within a week. Marceline brightened up perceptibly, though not without a venomous look at me. It seemed as if her coiled hair visibly tightened about her head.

"'I'm to be the first to see it!' she snapped. Then, smiling at Marsh, she added, 'And if I don't like it I shall slash it to pieces!'

"Marsh's face took on the most curious look I had ever seen it wear as he answered her.

"'I can't vouch for your taste, Marceline, but I swear it will be magnificent! Not that I want to take much credit—art creates itself—and this thing had to be done. Just wait!'

"During the next few days I felt a queer sense of foreboding, as if the completion of the picture meant a kind of catastrophe instead of a relief. Denis, too, had not written me, and my agent in New York said he was planning some trip to the country. I wondered what the outcome of the whole thing would be. What a queer mixture of elements—Marsh and Marceline, Denis and I! How would all these ultimately react on one another? When my fears grew too great I tried to lay them all to my infirmity, but that explanation never quite satisfied me.

"Well, the thing exploded on Tuesday, the 26th of August. I had risen at my usual time and had breakfast, but was not good for much because of the pain in my spine. It had been troubling me badly of late, and forcing me to take opiates when it got too unbearable; nobody else was downstairs except the servants, though I could hear Marceline moving about in her room. Marsh slept in the attic next his studio, and had begun to keep such late hours that he was seldom up till noon. About ten o'clock the pain got the better of me, so that I took a double dose of my opiate and lay down on the parlor sofa. The last I heard was Marceline's pacing overhead. Poor creature—if I had known! She must have been walking before the long mirror admiring herself. That was like her—vain from start to finish, reveling in her own beauty, just as she reveled in all the little luxuries Denis was able to give her.

"I didn't wake up till near sunset, and knew instantly how long I had slept from the golden light and long shadows outside the window. Nobody was about, and a sort of unnatural stillness seemed to be hovering over everything. From afar, though,

I thought I could sense a faint howling, wild and intermittent, whose quality had a slight but baffling familiarity about it. I'm not much for psychic premonitions, but I was frightfully uneasy from the start. There had been dreams, even worse than the ones I had been dreaming in the weeks before; and this time they seemed hideously linked to some black and festering reality. The whole place had a poisonous air. Afterward I reflected that certain sounds must have filtered through to my unconscious brain during those hours of drugged sleep. My pain, though, was very much eased, and I rose and walked without difficulty.

"Soon enough I began to see that something was wrong. Marsh and Marceline might have been riding, but someone ought to have been getting dinner in the kitchen. Instead there was only silence, except for that faint distant howl or wail, and nobody answered when I pulled the old-fashioned bell-cord to summon Scipio. Then, chancing to look up, I saw the spreading stain on the ceiling—the bright red stain, that must have come through the floor of Marceline's room.

"In an instant I forgot my crippled back and hurried upstairs to find out the worst. Everything under the sun raced through my mind as I struggled with the dampness-warped door of that silent chamber, and most hideous of all was a terrible sense of malign fulfilment and fatal expectedness. I had, it struck me, known all along that nameless horrors were gathering; that something profoundly evil had gained a foothold under my roof from which only blood and tragedy could result.

"The door gave at last, and I stumbled into the large room beyond—all dim from the branches of the great trees outside the windows. For a moment I could do nothing but flinch at the faint evil odor that immediately struck my nostrils. Then, turning on the electric light and glancing around, I glimpsed a nameless blasphemy on the yellow and blue rug.

"It lay face down in a great pool of dark, thickened blood, and had the gory print of a shod human foot in the middle of its naked back. Blood was spattered everywhere—on the walls, furniture and floor. My knees gave way as I took in the sight, so that I had to stumble to a chair and slump down. The thing had obviously been a human being, though its identity was not easy to establish at first, since it was without clothes and had most of its hair hacked and torn from the scalp in a very crude way. It was of a deep ivory color, and I knew that it must have been Marceline. The shoeprint on the back made the thing seem all the more hellish. I could not even picture the strange, loathsome tragedy which must have taken place while I slept in the room below. When I raised my hand to wipe my dripping forehead I saw that my fingers were sticky with blood. I shuddered, then realized that it must have come from the knob of the door which the unknown murderer had forced shut behind him as he left. He had taken his weapon with him, it seemed, for no instrument of death was visible here.

"As I studied the floor I saw that a line of sticky footprints like the one on the body led away from the horror to the door. There was another blood-trail, too, and of a less easily explainable kind; a broadish, continuous line, as if marking the path of some huge snake. At first I concluded it must be due to something the murderer had dragged after him. Then, noting the way some of the footprints seemed to be superimposed on it, I was forced to believe that it had been there when the murderer left. But what crawling entity could have been in that room with the victim and her assassin, leaving before the killer when the deed was done? As I asked myself this question, I thought I heard fresh bursts of that faint, distant wailing.

"Finally, rousing myself from a lethargy of horror, I got on my feet again and began following the footprints. Who the murderer was, I could not even faintly guess, nor could I try to explain the absence of the servants. I vaguely felt that I ought to go up to Marsh's attic quarters, but before I had fully formulated the idea I saw that the bloody trail was indeed taking me there. Was he himself the murderer? Had he gone mad under the strain of the morbid situation and suddenly run amok?

"In the attic corridor the trail became faint, the prints almost ceasing as they merged with the dark carpet. I could still, however, discern the strange single path of the entity which had gone first, and this led straight to the closed door of Marsh's studio, disappearing beneath it at a point about halfway from side to side. Evidently it had crossed the threshold at a time when the door was wide open.

"Sick at heart, I tried the knob and found the door unlocked. Opening it, I paused in the waning north light to see what fresh nightmare might be waiting me. There was certainly something human on the floor, and I reached for the switch to turn on the chandelier.

"But as the light flashed up, my gaze left the floor and its horror—that was Marsh, poor devil!—to fix itself frantically and incredulously upon the living thing that cowered and stared in the open doorway leading to Marsh's bedroom. It was a tousled, wild-eyed thing, crusted with the dried blood and carrying in its hand a wicked machete which had been one of the ornaments of the studio wall. Yet even in that awful moment I recognized it as one whom I had thought more than a thousand miles away. It was my own boy Denis—or the maddened wreck which had once been Denis.

"The sight of me seemed to bring back a trifle of sanity—or at least of memory—in the poor boy. He straightened up and began to toss his head about as if trying to shake free from some enveloping influence. I could not speak a word, but moved my lips in an effort to get back my voice. My eyes wandered for a moment to the figure on the floor in front of the heavily draped easel—the figure toward which the strange blood-trail led, and which seemed to be tangled in the coils of some dark, ropy object. The shifting of my glance apparently produced some impression in the twisted brain of the boy, for suddenly he began to mutter in a hoarse whisper, the purport of which I was soon able to catch.

"'I had to exterminate her—she was the devil!—the summit of high-priestess of all evil—the spawn of the pit—Marsh knew, and tried to warn me. Good old Frank! I didn't kill him, though I was ready to before I realized. But I went down there and killed her—then that cursed hair—'

"I listened in horror as Denis choked, paused, and began again.

"'You didn't know—her letters got queer and I knew she was with Marsh. Then she nearly stopped writing. He never mentioned her—I felt something was wrong, and thought I ought to come back and find out. Couldn't tell you—your manner would have given it away. Wanted to surprise them. Got here about noon today—came in a cab and sent the house-servants all off—let the field hands alone, for their cabins are all out of earshot. Told McCabe to get me some things in Cape Girardeau and not bother to come back till tomorrow. Had all the niggers take the old car and let Mary drive them to Bend Village for a vacation—told 'em we were all going on some sort of outing and wouldn't need help. Said they'd better stay all night with Uncle Scip's cousin, who keeps that nigger boarding-house.'

"Denis was getting very coherent now, and I strained my ears to grasp every word. Again I thought I heard that wild, far-off wail, but the story had first place for the present.

"'Saw you sleeping in the parlor, and took a chance you wouldn't wake up. Then went upstairs on the quiet to hunt up Marsh and—that woman!'

"The boy shuddered as he avoided pronouncing Marceline's name. At the same time I saw his eyes dilate in unison with a bursting of the distant crying, whose vague familiarity had now become very great.

"'She was not in her room, so I went up to the studio. Door was shut, and I could hear voices inside. Didn't knock—just burst in and found her posing for the picture. Nude, but with that hellish hair all draped around her. And making all sorts of sheep's-eyes at Marsh. He had the easel turned half away from the door, so I couldn't see the picture. Both of them were pretty well jolted when I showed up, and Marsh dropped his brush. I was in a rage and told him he'd have to show me the portrait, but he got calmer every minute—told me it wasn't quite done, but would be in a day or two—said I could see it then—she hadn't seen it.

"'But that didn't go with me. I stepped up, and he dropped a velvet curtain over the thing before I could see it. He was ready to fight before letting me see it, but that—that—she—stepped up and sided with me. Said we ought to see it. Frank got horribly worked up, and gave me a punch when I tried to get at the curtain. I punched back and seemed to have knocked him out. Then I was almost knocked out myself by the shriek that—that creature—gave. She'd drawn aside the hangings herself, and had caught a look at what Marsh had been painting. I wheeled around and saw her rushing like mad out of the room. *Then I saw the picture.*'

"Madness flared up in the boy's eyes again as he got to this place, and I thought for a minute he was going to spring at me with his machete. But after a pause he partly steadied himself.

"'O God—that thing! Don't ever look at it! Burn it with the hangings around it and throw the ashes into the river! Marsh knew—and was warning me. He knew what it was—what that woman—that leopardess, or gorgon, or lamia, or whatever she was—actually represented. He'd tried to hint to me ever since I met her in his Paris studio, but it couldn't be told in words. I thought they all wronged her when they whispered horrors about her, but this picture has caught the whole secret—the whole monstrous background!

"'God, but Frank is an artist! That thing is the greatest piece of work any living soul has produced since Rembrandt! It's a crime to burn it, but it would be a greater crime to let it exist—just as it would have been an abhorrent sin to let that she-demon exist any longer. The minute I saw it I understood what she was, and what part she played in the frightful secret that has come down from the days of Cthulhu and the Elder Ones—the secret that was nearly wiped out when Atlantis sunk, but that kept half alive in hidden traditions and allegorical myths and furtive, midnight cult-practises. She was the real thing. It wasn't any fake. It would have been merciful if it had been a fake. It was the old, hideous shadow that philosophers never dared mention—the thing hinted of in the *Necronomicon* and symbolized in the Easter Island colossi.

"'She thought we couldn't see through—that the false front would hold till we had bartered away our immortal souls. And she was half right—she'd have got me in the end. She was only—waiting. But Frank—good old Frank—was too much for her. *He knew what it all meant, and painted it.* I don't wonder she shrieked and ran off when she saw it. It wasn't quite done, but God knows *enough was there.*

"'Then I knew I'd got to kill her—kill her, and everything connected with her. It was a taint that wholesome human blood couldn't bear. There was something else, too—but you'll never know that if you burn the picture without looking. I staggered down to her room with this machete that I got off the wall here, leaving Frank still knocked out. He was breathing, though, and I knew and thanked heaven that I hadn't killed him.

"'I found her in front of the mirror braiding that accursed hair. She turned on me like a wild beast, and began spitting out her hatred of Marsh. The fact that she'd been in love with him (and I knew she had) only made it worse. For a minute I couldn't move, and she came within an ace of completely hypnotizing me. Then I thought of the picture, and the spell broke. She saw the breaking in my eyes, and must have noticed the machete too. I never saw anything but a wild jungle beast look as she did then. She sprang for me with claws out like a leopard's, but I was too quick. I swung the machete, and it was all over.'

"Denis had to stop again there, and I saw the perspiration running down his forehead through the spattered blood. But in a moment he hoarsely resumed.

"'I said it was all over—but God! some of it had only just begun! I felt I had fought the legions of Satan, and put my foot on the back of the thing I had annihilated. *Then I saw that blasphemous braid of coarse black hair began to twist and squirm of itself.*

"'I might have known it. It was all in the old tales. That damnable hair had a life of its own, that couldn't be ended by killing the creature herself. I knew I'd have to burn it, so I started to hack it off with the machete. God, but it was devilish work! Tough—like iron wires—but I managed to do it. And it was loathsome the way the big braid writhed and struggled in my grasp.

"'About the time I had the last strand cut or pulled off I heard the eldritch wailing from behind the house. It's still going, off and on. I don't know what it is, but it must be something springing from this hellish business. It half seems like something I ought to know but can't quite place. It got my nerves the first time I heard it, and I dropped the severed braid in my fright. Then I got a worse fright, for in another second the braid had turned on me and began to strike venomously with one of its ends which had knotted itself up like a sort of grotesque head. I struck out with the machete, and it turned away. Then, when I had my breath again, I saw that the monstrous thing was crawling along the floor by itself like a great black snake. I couldn't do anything for a while, but when it vanished through the door I managed to pull myself together and stumble after it. I could follow the broad, bloody trail, and I saw it led upstairs. It brought me here—and may heaven curse me if I didn't see it through the doorway, striking at poor dazed Marsh like a maddened rattler as it had struck at me, finally coiling around him as a python would. He had begun to come to, but that abominable serpent thing got him before he was on his feet. I knew that all of that woman's hatred was behind it, but I hadn't the power to pull it off. I tried, but it was too much for me. Even the machete was no good—I couldn't swing it freely or it would have slashed Frank to pieces. So I saw those monstrous coils tighten—saw poor Frank crushed to death before my eyes—and all the time that awful faint howling came from somewhere beyond the fields.

"I saw those monstrous coils tighten—saw poor Frank crushed to death before my eyes."

"'That's all. I pulled the velvet cloth over the picture, and I hope it'll never be lifted. The thing must be burnt. I couldn't pry the coils off poor, dead Frank—they clung to him like a leech, and seemed to have lost their motion altogether. It's as if that snaky rope of hair had a kind of perverse fondness for the man it killed—it's clinging to him—embracing him. You'll have to burn poor Frank with it—but for God's sake don't forget to see it in ashes! That and the picture. They must both go. The safety of the world demands that they go!'

"Denis might have whispered more, but a fresh burst of distant wailing cut us short. For the first time we knew what it was, for a westerly veering wind brought articulate words at last. We ought to have known long before, since sounds much like it had often come from the same source. It was wrinkled Sophonisba, the ancient Zulu witchwoman who had fawned on Marceline, keening from her cabin in a way which crowned the horrors of this nightmare tragedy. We could both hear some of the things she howled, and knew that secret and primordial bonds linked this savage sorceress with that other inheritor of Elder secrets who had just been extirpated. Some of the words she used betrayed her closeness to demonic and palesgean traditions.

"'*Iä! Iä! Shub-Niggurath! Ya-R'lyeh! N'gagi n'bulu bwana n'lolo!* Ya, yo, pore Missy Tanit, pore Missy Isis! Marse Clooloo, come up outen de water an' git yo' chile—she done daid! She done daid! De har ain' got no missus no mo', Marse Clooloo. Ol' Sophy, she know! Ol' Sophy, she done got de black stone outen Big Zimbabwe in ol' Affriky! Ol' Sophy, she done dance in de moonshine roun' de crocodile-stone befo' de N'bangus cotch her and sell her to de ship folks! No mo' Tanit! No mo' Isis! No mo' witchwoman to keep de fire a-goin' in de big stone place! Ya, yo! *N'gagi 'bulu bwana m'lolo! Iä! Shub-Niggurath!* She daid! Ol' Sophy know!'

"That wasn't the end of the wailing, but it was all I could pay attention to. The expression on my boy's face showed that it had reminded him of something frightful, and the tightening of his hand on the machete boded no good. I knew he was desperate, and sprang to disarm him if possible before he could do anything more.

"But I was too late. An old man with a bad spine doesn't count for much physically. There was a struggle, but he had done for himself before many seconds were over. I'm not sure yet but that he tried to kill me, too. His last panting words were something about the need of wiping out everything that had ever been connected with Marceline, either by blood or marriage.

"I wonder to this day that I didn't go stark mad in that instant, or in the moments and hours afterward. In front of me was the slain body of my boy, the only human being I had to cherish, and ten feet away, in front of that shrouded easel, was the body of his best friend, with a nameless coil of horror wound around it. Below was the scalped corpse of that she-monster, about whom I was half ready to believe anything. I was too dazed to analyze the probability of the hair story, and even if I had not been, that dismal howling from Aunt Sophy's cabin would have been enough to quiet doubt.

"If I'd been wise, I'd have done just what poor Denis told me to—burned the picture and the body-grasping hair at once and without curiosity—but I was too shaken to be wise. I suppose I muttered foolish things over my boy—and then I remembered that the night was wearing on and that the servants would be back in the morning. It was plain that a matter like this could never be explained, and I knew that I must cover things up and invent a story.

"That coil of hair around Marsh was a monstrous thing. I didn't dare touch it, and the longer I looked at it the more horrible things I noticed about it. One thing gave me a start. I won't mention it, but it partly explained the need for feeding the hair with queer oils as Marceline had always done.

"In the end I decided to bury all three bodies in the cellar, with quicklime, which I knew we had in the storehouse. It was a night of hellish work. I dug three graves—my boy's a long way from the other two, for I didn't want him to be near either the woman's body or her hair. I was sorry I couldn't get the coil from around poor Marsh. It was terrible work getting them all down to the cellar. I used blankets in carting the woman and the poor devil with the coil around him. Then I had to get two barrels of lime from the storehouse. God must have given me strength, for I not only moved them both but filled all three graves without a hitch.

"Some of the lime I made into white-wash. I had to take a stepladder and fix over the parlor ceiling where the blood had oozed through. And I burned nearly everything in Marceline's room, scrubbing the walls and floor and heavy furniture. I washed up the attic studio, too, and the trail and footprints that led there. And all the time I could hear old Sophy's wailing in the distance. The devil must have been in that creature to let her voice go on like that. But she always was howling queer things. That's why the field niggers didn't get scared or curious that night. I locked the studio door and took the key to my room. Then I burned all my stained clothes in the fire-place. By dawn the whole house looked quite normal, so far as any casual eye could tell. I hadn't dared touch the covered easel, but meant to attend to that later.

"Well, the servants came back next day, and I told them all the young folks had gone to St. Louis. None of the field hands seemed to have seen or heard anything, and old Sophonisba's wailing had stopped at the instant of sunrise. She was like a sphinx after that, and never let out a word of what had been on her brooding witch-brain the day and night before.

"Later on I pretended that Denis and Marsh and Marceline had gone back to Paris and had a certain discreet agency mail me letters from there—letters I had fixed up in forged handwriting. I had the deaths of Marsh and Denis reported during the war, and later said Marceline had entered a convent. Fortunately Marsh was an orphan whose eccentric ways had alienated him from his people in Louisiana. Things might have been patched up a good deal better for me if I had had the sense to burn the picture, sell the plantation, and give up trying to manage things with a shaken and overstrained mind. You see what my folly has brought me to. Failing crops, hands discharged one by one, place falling to ruin, and myself a hermit and a target for dozens of queer countryside stories. Nobody will come around here after dark nowadays—or any other time if it can be helped. That's why I knew you must be a stranger.

"And why do I stay here? I can't wholly tell you that. It's bound up too closely with things at the very rim of sane reality. It wouldn't have been so, perhaps, if I hadn't looked at the picture. I ought to have done as poor Denis told me. I honestly meant to burn it when I went up to that locked studio a week after the horror, but I looked first—and that changed everything.

"No—there's no use telling what I saw. You can, in a way, see for yourself presently; though time and dampness have done their work. I don't think it can hurt you if you want to take a look, but it was different with me. I knew too much of what it all meant.

"Denis had been right—it was the greatest triumph of human art since Rembrandt, even though still unfinished. I grasped that at the start, and knew that poor Marsh had justified his decadent philosophy. He was to painting what Baudelaire was to poetry, and Marceline was the key that had unlocked his inmost genius.

"The thing almost stunned me when I pulled aside the hangings—stunned me before I half knew what the whole thing was. You know, it's only partly a portrait. Marsh had been pretty literal when he hinted that he wasn't painting Marceline alone, but what he saw through her and beyond her.

"Of course she was in it—was the key to it, in a sense—but her figure only formed one point in a vast composition. She was nude except for that hideous web of hair spun around her, and was half seated, half reclining on a sort of bench or divan, carved in patterns unlike those of any known decorative tradition. There was a monstrously shaped goblet in one hand, from which was spilling fluid whose color I haven't been able to place or classify to this day.

"The figure and the divan were in the left-hand foreground of the strangest sort of scene I ever saw in my life. I think there was a faint suggestion of its all being a kind of emanation from the woman's brain; yet there was also a directly opposite suggestion—as if she were just an evil image or hallucination conjured up by the scene itself.

"I can't tell you now whether it's an exterior or an interior, whether those hellish cyclopean vaultings are seen from the outside or the inside, or whether they are indeed carven stone and not merely a morbid fungous arborescence. The geometry of the whole thing is crazy—one gets the acute and obtuse angles all mixed up.

"And God! The shapes of nightmare that float around in that perpetual demon twilight! The blasphemies that lurk and leer and hold a witches' sabbat with that woman as a high priestess! The black shaggy entities that are not quite goats—the crocodile-headed beast with three legs and a dorsal row of tentacles—and the flat-nosed Ægipans dancing in a pattern that Egypt's priests knew and called accursed!

"But the scene wasn't Egypt—it was *behind* Egypt; behind even Atlantis; behind fabled Mu, and myth-whispered Lemuria. It was the ultimate fountainhead of all horror on this earth, and the symbolism showed only too clearly how integral a part of it Marceline was. I think it must be the unmentionable R'lyeh, that was not built by any creatures of our planet—the thing Marsh and Denis used to talk about in the shadows with hushed voices. In the picture it appears that the whole scene is deep under water, though everybody seems to be breathing freely.

"Well, I couldn't do anything but look and shudder, and finally I saw that Marceline was watching me craftily out of those monstrous, dilated eyes on the canvas. It was no mere superstition—Marsh had actually caught something of her horrible vitality in his symphonies of line and color; so that she still brooded and stared and hated, just as if most of her weren't down in the cellar under quicklime. *And it was worst of all when some of those Hecate-born snaky strands of hair began to lift themselves up from the surface and grope out into the room toward me!*

"Then it was that I knew the last final horror, and realized I was a guardian and a prisoner for ever. She was the thing from which the first dim legends of Medusa and the Gorgons had sprung, and something in my shaken will had been captured and turned to stone at last. Never again would I be safe from those coiling snaky strands—the strands in the picture, and those that lay brooding under the lime near the wine casks. All too late I recalled the tales of the virtual indestructibility, even through centuries of burial, of the hair of the dead.

"My life since has been nothing but horror and slavery. Always there has lurked the fear of what broods down in the cellar. In less than a month the niggers began whispering about the great black snake that crawled around near the wine casks after dark, and about the curious way its trail would lead to another spot six feet away. Finally I had to move everything to another part of the cellar, for not a darky could be induced to go near the place where the snake was seen.

"Then the field hands began talking about the black snake that visited old Sophonisba's cabin every night after midnight. One of them showed me its trail, and not long afterward I found out that Aunt Sophy herself had begun to pay strange visits to the cellar of the big house, lingering and muttering for hours in the very spot where none of the other blacks would go. God, but I was glad when that old witch died! I honestly believe she had been a priestess of some ancient and terrible tradition back in Africa. She must have lived to be almost a hundred and fifty years old.

"Sometimes I think I hear something gliding around the house at night. There will be a queer noise on the stairs, where the boards are loose, and the latch of my room will rattle as if with an inward pressure. I always keep my door locked, of course. Then there are certain mornings when I seem to catch a sickish musty odor in the corridors, and notice a faint, ropy trail through the dust of the floors. I know I must guard the hair in the picture, for if anything were to happen to it, there are entities in this house which would take a sure and terrible revenge. I don't even dare to die; for life and death are all one to those in the clutch of what came out of R'lyeh. Something would be on hand to punish my neglect. Medusa's coil has got me, and it will always be the same. Never mix up with secret and ultimate horror, young man, if you value your immortal soul."

As the old man finished his story I saw that the small lamp had long since burned dry, and that the large one was nearly empty. It must, I knew, be near dawn; and my ears told me that the storm was over. The tale had held me in a half-daze, and I almost feared to glance at the door lest it reveal an inward pressure from some unnameable source. It would be hard to say which had the greatest hold on me—stark horror, incredulity, or a kind of morbid fantastic curiosity. I was wholly beyond speech and had to wait for my strange host to break the spell.

"Do you want to see—the thing?"

His voice was very low and hesitant, and I saw he was tremendously in earnest. Of my various emotions, curiosity gained the upper hand, and I nodded silently. He rose, lighting a candle on a near-by table and holding it high before him as he opened the door.

"Come with me—upstairs."

I dreaded to brave those musty corridors again, but fascination downed all my qualms. The boards creaked beneath our feet, and I trembled once when I thought I saw a faint, rope-like line traced in the dust near the staircase.

The steps of the attic were noisy and rickety, with several of the treads missing. I was glad of the need of looking sharply to my footing, for it gave me an excuse not to glance about. The attic corridor was pitch-black and heavily cobwebbed, and inch-deep with dust except where a beaten trail led to a door on the left at the farther end. As I noticed the rotting remains of a thick carpet, I thought of the other feet which had pressed it in bygone decades—of these, and of one thing which did not have feet.

The old man took me straight to the door at the end of the beaten path, and fumbled a second with the rusty latch. I was acutely frightened now that I knew the picture was so close, yet dared not retreat at this stage. In another moment my host was ushering me into the deserted studio.

The candlelight was very faint, yet served to show most of the principal features. I noticed the low, slanting roof, the huge enlarged dormer, the curios and trophies hung on the walls, and most of all, the great shrouded easel in the center of the floor. To that easel de Russy now walked, drawing aside the dusty velvet hangings on the side turned away from me, and motioning me silently to approach. It took a good deal of courage to make me obey, especially when I saw how my guide's eyes dilated in the wavering candlelight as he looked at the unveiled canvas. But again curiosity conquered everything, and I walked around to where de Russy stood. Then I saw the damnable thing.

I did not faint, though no reader can possibly realize the effort it took to keep me from doing so. I did cry out, but stopped short when I saw the frightened look on the old man's face. As I had expected, the canvas was warped, moldy, and scabrous from dampness and neglect; but for all that I could trace the monstrous hints of evil cosmic outsideness that lurked all through the nameless scene's morbid content and perverted geometry.

It was as the old man had said: a vaulted, columned hell of mingled Black Masses and witches' sabbats, and what perfect completion could have added to it was beyond my power to guess. Decay had only increased the utter hideousness of its wicked symbolism and diseased suggestion; for the parts most affected by time were just these parts of the picture which in nature—or in that extra-cosmic realm that mocked nature—would be likely to decay or disintegrate.

The utmost horror of all, of course, was Marceline; and as I saw the bloated, discolored flesh I formed the odd fancy that perhaps the figure on the canvas had some obscure, occult linkage with the figure which lay in quicklime under the cellar floor. Perhaps the lime had preserved the corpse instead of destroying it—but could it have preserved those black, malign eyes that glared and mocked at me from their painted hell?

And there was something else about the creature which I could not fail to notice—something which de Russy had not been able to put into words, but which perhaps had something to do with Denis' wish to kill all those of his blood who had dwelt under the same roof with her. Whether Marsh knew, or whether the genius in him painted it without his knowing, none could say. But Denis and his father could not have known till they saw the picture.

Surpassing all in horror was the streaming black hair, which covered the rotting body, *but which was itself not even slightly decayed.* All I had heard of it was amply verified. It was nothing human, this ropy, sinuous, half-oily, half-crinkly flood of serpent darkness. Vile, independent life proclaimed itself at every unnatural twist and convolution, and the suggestion of numberless *reptilian* heads at the out-turned ends was far too marked to be illusory or accidental.

The blasphemous thing held me like a magnet. I was helpless, and did not wonder at the myth of the gorgon's glance which turned all beholders to stone. Then I thought I saw a change come over the thing. The leering features perceptibly moved, so that the rotting jaw fell, allowing the thick, beast-like lips to disclose a row of pointed yellow fangs. The pupils of the fiendish eyes dilated, and the eyes themselves seemed to bulge outward. And the hair—that accursed hair! *It had begun to rustle and wave perceptibly, the snake-heads all turning toward de Russy and vibrating as if to strike!*

Reason deserted me altogether, and before I knew what I was doing I drew my revolver and sent a shower of six steel-jacketed bullets through the shocking canvas. The whole thing at once fell to pieces, even the frame toppling from the easel and clattering to the dust-covered floor. But though this horror was shattered, another had risen before me in the form of de Russy himself, whose maddened shrieks as he saw the picture vanish were almost as terrible as the picture itself had been.

With a half-articulate scream of "God, now you've done it!" the frantic old man seized me violently by the arm and commenced to drag me out of the room and down the rickety stairs. He had dropped the candle in his panic, but dawn was near, and some faint gray light was filtering in through the dust-covered windows. I tripped and stumbled repeatedly, but never for a moment would my guide slacken his pace.

"Run!" he shrieked, "run for your life! You don't know what you've done! I never told you the whole thing! There were things I had to do—*the picture talked to me and told me.* I had to guard and keep it—now the worst will happen! *She and that hair will come up out of their graves, for God knows what purpose!*

"Hurry, man! For God's sake let's get out of here while there's time. If you have a car, take me along to Cape Girardeau with you. It may get me in the end, anywhere, but I'll give it a run for its money. Out of here—quick!"

As we reached the ground floor I became aware of a slow, curious thumping from the rear of the house, followed by the sound of a door shutting. De Russy had not heard the thumping, but the other noise caught his ear and drew from him the most terrible shriek that ever sounded in human throat.

"Oh, God—great God—that was the cellar door—she's coming—"

By this time I was desperately wrestling with the rusty latch and sagging hinges of the great front door—almost as frantic as my host, now that I heard the slow, thumping tread approaching from the unknown rear rooms of the accursed mansion. The night's rain had warped the oaken planks, and the heavy door stuck and resisted even more strongly than it had when I forced an entrance the evening before.

Somewhere a plank creaked beneath the foot of whatever was walking, and the sound seemed to snap the last cord of sanity in the poor old man. With a roar like that of a maddened bull he released his grip on me and made a plunge to the right, through the open door of a room which I judged had been a parlor. A second later, just as I got the front door open and was making my own escape, I heard the tinkling clatter of broken glass and knew he had leapt through a window. And as I bounded off the sagging porch to commence my mad race down the long, weed-grown drive I thought I could catch the thud of dead, dogged footfalls which did not follow me, but which kept leadenly on through the door of the cobwebbed parlor.

I looked backward only twice as I plunged heedlessly through the burrs and briars of that abandoned drive, past the dying lindens and grotesque scrub-oaks, in the gray pallor of a cloudy November dawn. The first time was when an acrid smell overtook me, and I thought of the candle de Russy had dropped in the attic studio. By then I was comfortably near the road, on the high place from which the roof of the distant house was clearly visible above its encircling trees; and just as I expected, thick clouds of smoke were billowing out of the attic dormers and curling upward into the leaden heavens. I thanked the powers of creation that an immemorial curse was about to be purged by fire and blotted from the earth.

But in the next instant came that second backward look in which I glimpsed two other things—things that canceled most of the relief and gave me a supreme shock from which I shall never recover. I have said that I was on a high part of the drive, from which much of the plantation behind me was visible. This vista included not only the house and its trees but some of the abandoned and partly flooded flat land beside the river, and several bends of the weed-choked drive I had been so hastily traversing. In both of these latter places I now beheld sights—or suspicions of sights—which I wish devoutly I could deny.

It was a faint, distant scream which made me turn back again, and as I did so I caught a trace of motion on the dull gray marshy plain behind the house. At that distance human figures are very small; yet I thought the motion resolved itself into two of these, pursuer and pursued. I even thought I saw the dark-clothed leading figure overtaken and seized by the bald, naked figure in the rear—overtaken, seized, and dragged violently in the direction of the now burning house.

But I could not watch the outcome, for at once a nearer sight obtruded itself—a suggestion of motion among the underbrush at a point some distance back along the deserted drive. Unmistakably, the weeds and bushes and briars were swaying as no wind could sway them; swaying as if some large, swift serpent were wriggling purposefully along on the ground in pursuit of me.

That was all I could stand. I scrambled along madly for the gate, heedless of torn clothing and bleeding scratches, and jumped into the roadster parked under the great evergreen tree. It was a bedraggled, rain-drenched sight, but the works were unharmed and I had no trouble in starting the thing. I went on blindly in the direction the car was headed for. Nothing was in my mind but to get away from that frightful region of nightmares and cacodemons—to get away as quickly and as far as gasoline could take me.

About three or four miles along the road a farmer hailed me—a kindly, drawling fellow of middle age and considerable native intelligence. I was glad to slow down and ask directions, though I knew I must present a strange enough aspect. The man readily told me the way to Cape Girardeau, and inquired where I had come from in such a state at such an early hour. Thinking it best to say little, I merely mentioned that I had been caught in the night's rain and had taken shelter at a near-by farmhouse, afterward losing my way in the underbrush trying to find my car.

"At a farmhouse, eh? Wonder whose it coulda ben. Ain't nothin' standin' this side o' Jim Ferris' place acrost Barker's Crick, an' that's all o' twenty miles by the rud."

I gave a start, and wondered what fresh mystery this portended, then asked my informant if he had overlooked the large ruined plantation house whose ancient gate bordered the road not far back.

"Funny ye sh'd recolleck that, stranger! Musta ben here afore sometime. But that house ain't there now. Burnt down five or six years ago—and they did tell some queer stories about it."

I shuddered.

"You mean Riverside—ol' man de Russy's place. Queer goin's on there fifteen or twenty years ago. Ol' man's boy married a gal from abroad, and some folks thought she was a mighty odd sort. Didn't like the looks of her. Then she and the boy went off sudden, and later on the ol' man said he was kilt in the war. But some o' the niggers hinted queer things. Got around at last that the ol' fellow fell in love with the gal himself and kilt her and the boy. That place was sure enough ha'nted by a black snake, mean that what it may.

"Then five or six years ago the ol' man disappeared and the house burned down. Some do say he was burnt up in it. It was a mornin' after a rainy night just like this, when lots o' folks heard an awful yellin' acrost the fields in ol' de Russy's voice. When they stopped and looked, they see the house goin' up in smoke quick as a wink—that place was all like tinder anyhow, rain or no rain. Nobody never seen the ol' man agin, but onct in a while they tell of the ghost of that big black snake glidin' aroun'.

"What d'you make of it, anyhow? You seem to hev knowed the place. Didn't ye ever hear tell of the de Russys? What d'ye reckon was the trouble with that gal young Denis married? She kinder made everybody shiver and feel hateful, though ye couldn't never tell why."

I was trying to think, but that process was almost beyond me now. The house burned years ago? Then where, and under what conditions, had I passed the night? And why did I know what I knew of these things? Even as I pondered I saw a hair on my coat sleeve—the short, gray hair of an old man.

In the end I drove on without telling anything. But I did hint that gossip was wronging the poor old planter who had suffered so much. I made it clear—as if from distant but authentic reports wafted among friends—that if anyone was to blame for the trouble at Riverside it was the woman, Marceline. She was not suited to Missouri ways, I said, and it was too bad that Denis had ever married her.

More I did not intimate, for I felt that the de Russys, with their proudly cherished honor and high, sensitive spirits, would not wish me to say more. They had borne enough, God knows, without the countryside guessing what a demon of the pit, what a gorgon of the Elder blasphemies, had come to flaunt their ancient and stainless name.

Nor was it right that the neighbors should know that other horror which my strange host of the night could not bring himself to tell me—that horror which he must have learned as I learned it, from details in the lost masterpiece of poor Frank Marsh.

It would be too hideous if they knew that the one-time heiress of Riverside—the accursed gorgon or lamia whose hateful crinkly coil of serpent-hair must even now be brooding and twining vampirically around an artist's skeleton in a lime-packed grave beneath a charred foundation—was faintly, subtly, yet unmistakably the scion of Zimbabwe's most primal grovelers. No wonder she owned a link with the old witchwoman Sophonisba—for, though in deceitfully slight proportion, Marceline was a loathsome, bestial thing, and her forebears had come from Africa.